Amount	Sunshine in last 4 hours	Thunder & Lightning	Rain/Snow/Hail	Daily Rain Gauge Reading	The Weather Now			
covered in eighths)					Halo round Moon			
	☼							
	☼				Clouds getting lower and thicker	Warm Front Approaching ?		Probably rain coming but should get warmer.
4/8								
4/8				↓				
4/8			🌧	2 mm				
4/8			🌧		Drizzle	Warm Front arrives		
6/8			🌧		Heavy rain		changeable Day!	
2/8	☼				Clearing rapidly. Warm Sector			
6/8			🌧		More Rain!	Cold Front arrives		
4/8				↓				
				21 mm	Sky clearing			Expect clearer cooler weather
	☼							
1/8	☼	⚡	Hail!		Short Thunder Showers	Into Cold Sector ↓		

D I A R Y

Nowadays, satellites and very powerful computers are used in Meteorology — the science of the weather — and it is usually boys and girls who enjoy mathematics and physics who study to become meteorologists. These may not be your favourite subjects, but you can still become quite skilful at forecasting what the weather will do next.

All you need is your eyes and a few simple instruments. This book shows you how.

Acknowledgments:
The author and publishers wish to thank the following for use of illustrative material:
Armagh Planetarium, page 43; Austin J Brown, Aviation Picture Library, page 24; Camera Press, page 34; Canadian High Commission, page 7; Tim Clark, pages 22 and 35 (bottom); Bruce Coleman, page 17 (top right and bottom right), 20, 32(3) and 33; Crown copyright — pages 50 and 51 reproduced with the permission of the Controller, HMSO; Daily Telegraph, page 15 (bottom); Drury Lane Studios, front endpaper and pages 5, 6, 12, 29, 31 and 33; J H Golden, page 17 (bottom left); Terry Hope, page 41 (top); Irridelco (UK) Ltd, page 21; Ian Morrison (author), pages 4, 10, 11, 13, 15 (top), 18, 19(2), 30, 37, 40 and 49; Rob Norman, pages 8, 9, 25, 36, 38, 39, 42, 44/5 and 46/7; Space and New Concepts Department, RAE Farnborough, pages 16, 48 and 49 (bottom); Harry Stanton, title page, 26, 27(2), 28 and 41 (bottom); G H Zeal Ltd, pages 6 and 23.

British Library Cataloguing in Publication Data

Morrison, Ian A.
   Weather. — (Ladybird science)
   1. Weather — Juvenile literature
  I. Title   II. Series
  551.5   QC981.3

  ISBN 0-7214-0825-7

First edition

© LADYBIRD BOOKS LTD MCMLXXXV

Weather

by IAN A. MORRISON, M A, Ph D.

Ladybird Books Loughborough

There was once a law that weather prophets should be put to death as witches. That was back in the 16th century, when foretelling future events seemed to need magical powers. Nowadays, we realise that by studying the patterns of past weather and taking observations with instruments, we can make forecasts by working scientifically.

One of the best ways to understand how professional meteorologists do this is to have a go at running your own weather station. You can become quite a successful forecaster using very simple equipment. Even today the professionals still rely on uncomplicated instruments such as thermometers. Indeed, in our present era of weather satellites and computers, it is rather nice to find some of them still use a device that looks remarkably like the crystal balls by which story-book fortune tellers were supposed to foretell the future! The glass ball acts as a lens. This focuses the sun to char a track on a strip of paper, recording the hours of sunshine.

A Campbell-Stokes sunshine recorder

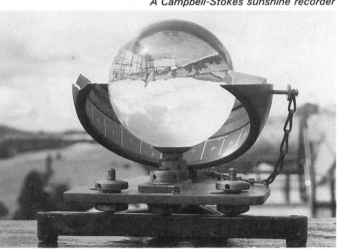

The sun is the main key to our weather, wherever we live on Earth. The word *climate* is used to sum up what the weather is usually like at a particular place, and our planet has a great variety of climates because of the different ways that the sun's energy affects it. We are used to the idea of the North and South Poles being icy places, and the part of the globe midway between them, around the Equator, being hot. This is because the sunlight beats down almost directly in the Tropics near the Equator,

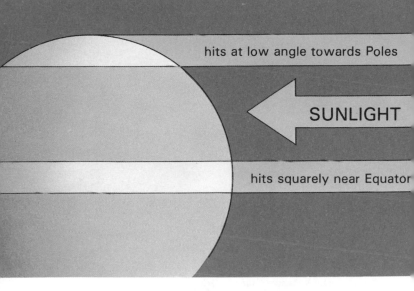

hits at low angle towards Poles

SUNLIGHT

hits squarely near Equator

whereas it just glances past the top and bottom of the globe.

Some of the sunlight that does reach the Polar Regions is lost back into space because the white snow there is a good reflector. So almost two and a half times as much energy from the sun is available at the Equator as at the Poles.

That's how things average out over the year, but there are contrasts between summer and winter, as the Earth travels in its year-long orbit round the sun. This is because the planet is tilted, with the line through the Poles on which the Earth is spinning leaning over at 66.5 degrees. This means that for half of each round trip, the north of the planet is tilted away from the sun. That gives

Northern Winter   **Northern Summer**

Southern Summer   **Southern Winter**
(The Sun is much bigger and the distances are much greater than can be shown here.)

it shorter days and brings its winter, while the south is benefiting from longer days and enjoying summer.

Then, as the planet sweeps round to the other side of the sun, the seasons change and the tilt gives the south its winter, while the north heats up for its summer. So Christmas is hot in Australasia or South Africa, but cold in North America or the UK.

As the seasons change, some parts of the planet heat up and cool down more quickly than others. Mountains or lowlands, forests or deserts, all behave differently. But the most basic contrast in temperature is between land and water. Seas and oceans vary slowly, because it takes a long time for changes above them to affect deeper water.

Land surfaces respond more rapidly. So inside a big continent, the heat builds up in the summer. But it gets really cold in winter, too. Winter in Russia is freezing cold, but in maritime Scotland, fur hats are not needed. Yet Moscow is actually further south than Edinburgh! North America shows these continental effects strongly

Summer in the city of Toronto, on the Great Lakes

too, though the Great Lakes are big enough to help to cool down the summers and to off-set some of the winter cold. From this you might think that wherever you lived by an ocean, summers would be cooler and winters warmer than if you lived inland. This is usually but not always so, because the water, as well as the air of the planet, is on the move. The climate on some coasts is influenced by ocean currents that bring water that has been warmed or chilled elsewhere.

The Labrador Current brings Arctic water and even icebergs far south, chilling the east coast of Canada. But on the west coast of Europe, the climate is quite different. The North Atlantic Drift carries water right across the ocean from the warm Gulf Stream, which starts thousands of kilometres to the south. Tropical turtles have reached Shetland, the most northerly part of Britain. There are only a few days of snow in most years there, yet Shetland lies as far north as part of Greenland, and is nearer to the North Pole than such snowy places as Churchill on Hudson Bay or Juneau in Alaska.

In Australia, the kind of weather that you get if you live by the sea is affected by whether you are on the east coast, where warm currents come southwards, or on the west where cool waters move north. And in the Outback, hundreds of kilometres inland, temperatures go much higher than in the narrow southern island of New Zealand, surrounded by its cool seas.

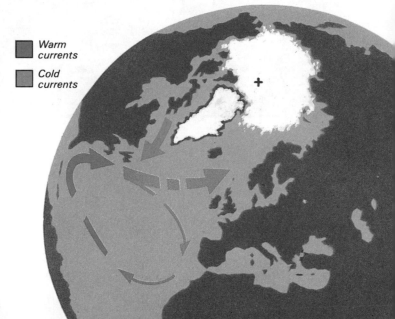

Warm currents

Cold currents

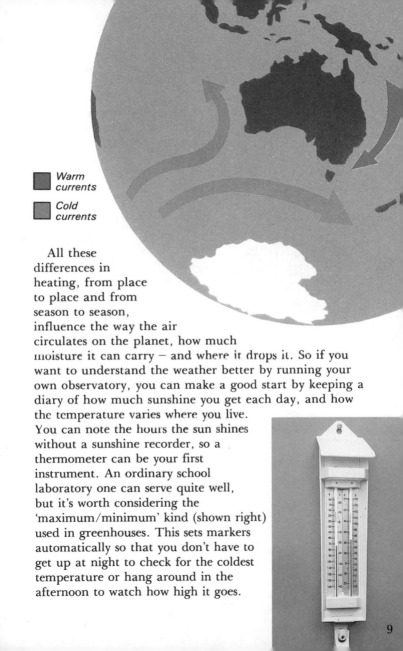

Warm currents

Cold currents

All these differences in heating, from place to place and from season to season, influence the way the air circulates on the planet, how much moisture it can carry — and where it drops it. So if you want to understand the weather better by running your own observatory, you can make a good start by keeping a diary of how much sunshine you get each day, and how the temperature varies where you live. You can note the hours the sun shines without a sunshine recorder, so a thermometer can be your first instrument. An ordinary school laboratory one can serve quite well, but it's worth considering the 'maximum/minimum' kind (shown right) used in greenhouses. This sets markers automatically so that you don't have to get up at night to check for the coldest temperature or hang around in the afternoon to watch how high it goes.

As air gets warmer, it tends to expand and become less dense. So cold air is heavier than warm air. Barometers measure the pressure that different weights of air exert. Inside the kind called an *aneroid* is a metal box that has been emptied of air. Only the springiness of the metal stops it from collapsing altogether under the pressure of the atmosphere. It is squashed more on days when the

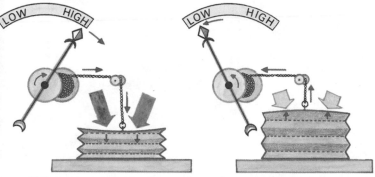

High pressure squeezes box, pulls pointer to right.

Low pressure lets box expand, pointer returns to left.

pressure is higher, and recovers as pressure becomes lower. This movement works a pointer, showing the changes on a dial. Many families already have a barometer, because it can give a good idea of what the weather may do next. The dial may be marked 'Fair' and 'Stormy', but these markings are often misleading. It is not so much where the

hand points as the way that it is moving which gives the best clues to forecasters. Some barometers have a pen on the pointer that records pressure movements on a drum driven by a clock (*left*), but you don't need one of those. You can keep track of the main changes quite easily by taking readings regularly each day (say at breakfast, lunch and bedtime). Note them in your weather diary. If you can do graphs, draw them with 'time' running across the page, to show 'pressure' moving up and down.

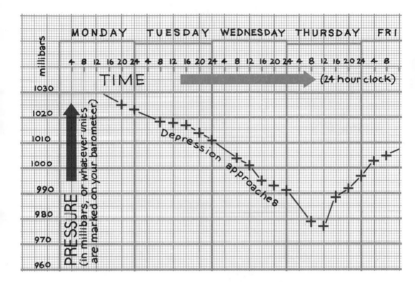

Just as the way different parts of the planet are heated influences the pattern of high and low pressure areas, so in turn, the pressure pattern affects how the winds blow. Cold regions like the Arctic and Antarctic tend to be areas of high pressure since they are covered with caps of heavy chilled air. This sinks and spreads outwards, giving cold winds which blow towards warmer low pressure areas. Equally, the air heated in the hot zones of the Earth expands, becomes lighter, and rises. This uprising air has to be replaced at ground level, so air is drawn sideways into the low pressure zones created there.

You might think that this would give a simple weather pattern to the planet, with winds blowing directly from the high pressure of the cold Polar Regions to the hot belt along the Equator. But remember that the Earth is spinning on its axis; that is, the line through the North and South Poles. This means that if air left the North Pole heading directly south, by the time it reached Shetland or southern Hudson Bay (both a third of the way to the Equator), it would be travelling over land and sea which is rushing eastwards at nearly 840 kph. Two-thirds of the way to the Equator, the speed is nearly 1,500 kph. That's where Florida and Texas lie in the north of the planet, and much of South Africa or the great Nullarbor Plain of Australia lie in the southern half. At the Equator itself, the speed the Earth's surface is moving is around 1,675 kph. So instead of blowing directly from high pressure to low, winds are swung round. North of the

Speeds of Earth's surface

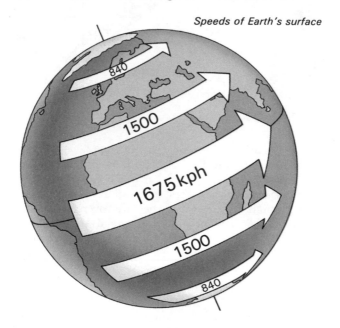

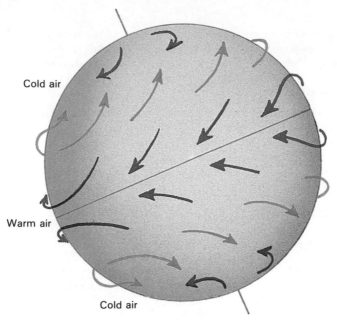

Cold air

Warm air

Cold air

Equator, they swirl anti-clockwise into a low pressure
area – so impress your friends that you are a great
meteorologist, by telling them where the low pressure lies
before you see the TV weather map (all you have to
remember is that it's on your left when you stand with
your back to the wind). But if you are south of the
Equator, the swirl due to the spin of the planet works the
other way round.

As we shall see later, the way winds change can tell us
quite a lot about what the weather is going to do. So if
you are going to try your hand at forecasting, it is a good
idea to record the wind direction and speed in your
weather diary. You can easily make a wind vane, and
borrow a compass of the kind used by orienteers or hill-
walkers to set it up to show the direction. But be careful
to choose a place clear of wind eddies from trees or
buildings, which might give misleading effects.

Most of the time, you'll find the wind blows from much the same direction: this is called the *prevailing wind*. You can find what it is at your own observatory by drawing a wind rose showing how many days in the year the wind blows from each direction.

The instruments called *anemometers* used to measure wind speeds are expensive, but you can do without them. Admiral Sir Francis Beaufort invented a good way of describing wind force by just watching what effects different strengths have on the sea. We've added things that can be seen inland:

Beaufort Scale

FORCE	STRENGTH	SPEED approx. max. speed kph	EFFECT
0	CALM	0 – 1	Sea like mirror; smoke rises vertically
1	LIGHT AIR	– 5	Slight ripples on sea; smoke drifts
2	LIGHT BREEZE	– 10	Glassy wavelets; wind felt on face; vane begins to move; leaves rustle
3	GENTLE BREEZE	– 20	Wavelets begin to break; twigs moving; light flags unfurl
4	MODERATE BREEZE	– 30	'White horses' common; dust and loose paper blow about; small branches move
5	FRESH BREEZE	– 40	Medium sea waves; wavelets with crests on inland ponds; leafy shrubs sway
6	STRONG BREEZE	– 50	Large sea waves; big branches move; wires whistle; problems with umbrellas
7	NEAR GALE	– 60	Foam from breaking waves blown downwind; whole trees sway; walkers push into wind
8	GALE	– 75	Wave foam blown into long streaks; twigs break off trees; walking very hard
9	STRONG GALE	– 90	High waves, tumbling crests, thick spray; chimney pots, slates, branches blow down
10	STORM	– 100 +	White seas with very high waves; trees uprooted; bad damage to buildings

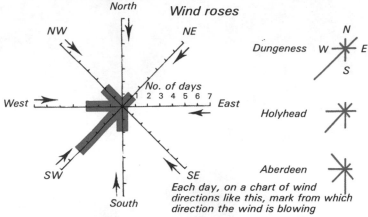

Wind roses

North
NW NE
No. of days
1 2 3 4 5 6 7
West — East
SW SE
South

Dungeness

N
W —✳— E
S

Holyhead

Aberdeen

Each day, on a chart of wind directions like this, mark from which direction the wind is blowing

By the time it's Force 12, it's full HURRICANE force! Such very powerful winds are created when the swirl of air going into a centre of low pressure spins faster and faster, in a rotating storm. These usually start over tropical oceans, and they are called Cyclones in the Indian Ocean, Typhoons in the China Seas, Willy-Willies off Australia, and Hurricanes in the Americas. As usual with winds drawn into low pressure, they turn anti-clockwise north of the Equator, but clockwise to the south.

Damage caused by a hurricane in the United States

15

Satellite photograph of a hurricane, showing the 'eye'

Hurricanes and their relatives show up dramatically in satellite photographs as a circular whirl of clouds, often over 500 km in diameter, racing round a small clear central hub: the 'Eye of the Storm'. It is towards the centre that you find winds of Beaufort Force 12 and over. Quite often speeds of more than 150 kph wreck houses and put ships in danger. The sea story *Typhoon* by Joseph Conrad gives a vivid idea of what it can be like. But within the clear Eye itself, it may be almost calm. So as the centre passes over, people have a short respite. This lull may last just for minutes or at most a few hours, before the storm suddenly returns in all its fury. This time the winds hit them from the opposite direction, as the opposite side of the wheel passes over them.

These huge circular storms are not the only swirls in the atmosphere that can be dangerous. Tornadoes are very much smaller, but inside them pressure may fall to half of what is normal. Windows and roofs explode outwards. The air spirals round in a narrow writhing

A tornado in Oklahoma, USA

column, often at speeds of over 150 kph, and sometimes possibly nearer 500 kph. Whole trees are twisted out of the ground, and even railway trucks weighing tonnes can be picked up. Happily, however, the trail of destruction that a tornado leaves is usually only about 100 m across. Parts of the American Mid-West and Australia suffer most, but tornadoes do occur very occasionally in Britain.

Dust-devils and water-spouts are spectacular but less dangerous. They happen where a tornado-like whirl sucks up sand or water. This is probably the explanation behind stories of it raining 'blood' (red dust carried from deserts far away) or indeed frogs (if not 'cats and dogs'!).

A water-spout in Florida, USA

A dust-devil in Namibia

17

Meteorologists can give general warnings about when tornadoes *might* occur (they usually happen when a mass of cold air pushes into warm air which is especially unstable and damp). But it is not really possible to know in advance exactly where such a local effect will strike. The same is true of the less dramatic events that make up our normal weather. It is much easier to forecast that 'showers are likely' than to foretell the exact place where a particular cloud will begin to drop rain. Most weather forecasting is in fact concerned with working out the broad patterns of what is likely to happen – we are doing quite well if we manage that!

To succeed, we want the measurements taken by all the weather stations to show up real differences in what is going on in the atmosphere, rather than just differences in the nature of the stations themselves. For instance, since pressure falls with height, a barometer at a station 5,500 m up a mountain would only show about half the reading at sea level. Pressure figures therefore have to be mathematically adjusted to take account of height above sea level. And thermometers in a black box that absorbed

A weather station

A Stevenson Screen

heat would show higher temperatures when the sun shone than others in a light-coloured box that reflected heat. Differing shelter from the wind would also affect temperature and dampness readings.

So that observations can be compared from station to station, meteorologists set instruments in a Stevenson Screen. This is called after the inventor, the father of Robert Louis Stevenson who wrote *Treasure Island*. It is a white painted box, with a double roof to keep off the sun, and slats in the side to baffle the wind. You could build one for your own observatory.

Inside a Stevenson Screen, showing wet and dry thermometers

Stevenson Screens are set at a standard height (1.2 m), so as not to be affected too much by what is going on at the ground surface. This certainly helps to give measurements that can be compared from station to station, to forecast what may happen next in the sky above. But we shouldn't turn our backs on the local effects that the Screen is designed to eliminate. We need to find out what *does* happen at ground level, since that affects our comfort and the lives of crops on which we depend. Try setting thermometers (the maximum/minimum kind if possible) just a couple of centimetres clear of the ground. The temperature there varies much more than in the shelter of the Screen. And since cold air sinks, the number of damaging frosts occurring down in the layer of air where plants grow is sometimes ten or

more times greater than up in the Screen – a good reason for storing potatoes on a shelf instead of the floor of the garden shed! Put thermometers close to different kinds of ground surfaces, and in sheltered and exposed places. Even within a small part of a town or countryside, it is remarkable how much conditions vary. You may find you can map routes where cold night air drains down steep streets, or collects in frost hollows.

Protecting oranges from frost with gas burners

Centre pivot irrigation, shown above and left, waters the ground in circles

Farmers and market gardeners have to avoid places like that. They sometimes find it pays them to ease the climate for their crops by planting shelter belts of trees, building greenhouses, or even burning gas out of doors to combat frost. And, of course, we ease the effect of the climate on ourselves by living in houses, and wearing clothes to match the weather. In many parts of the world, stored or transported water is used for irrigation, and there have even been attempts at rain-making by spraying chemicals into promising clouds.

Rain or clouds are visible, but air also holds moisture that we do not see, though we can often feel whether it is there. In dry air, when we perspire our sweat evaporates. That means it changes into water vapour, and as it dries up and disappears, we cool down. Provided we can get enough to drink, even high temperatures can thus be quite pleasant in the dry air of inland South Africa, Australia, or the American South West. But where the air is humid (nearly full of water vapour already), we stay hot and sticky. So hot swampy areas are uncomfortable places to live. But in cold climates, cooling by evaporation can actually kill you. That's why mountaineers carry 'survival bags' to crawl into in a storm. The light plastic is not warm in itself, but it stops their bodily moisture from getting carried off, and saves them from *wind chill*.

To get an idea of how much chance there is of rain coming on, it's useful to have a way of judging how full the air is of moisture.

There are toy houses, with a lady who appears when it's dry, and a man with an umbrella when it's rainy.

A strand of gut twists as the dampness of the air changes, moving them. But a better way of measuring humidity is to use this business of evaporation. If you've ever put one foot in a puddle, you'll know that compared to the dry one, that foot is kept horribly chilly by the wet sock. Instead of their feet, weathermen use two thermometers. One is kept dry, measuring air temperature in the usual way. The other wears a tiny cloth sock, kept wet by a wick from a dish of water (see photograph on page 19). If the air is very dry, water evaporates quickly so the wet thermometer shows a much lower reading than the dry one. But on a very humid day, nearly ready to rain, the amount of water vapour already in the air does not allow much evaporation to take place, so the two read almost the same. You could make up a 'wet-bulb' thermometer for yourself.

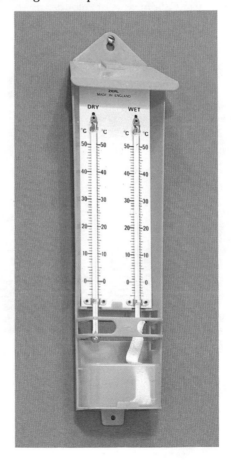

Wet and dry bulb thermometers

Warm air can carry a lot more moisture than cool air. So if anything causes the temperature of warm wet air to fall, it becomes unable to hold as much of its invisible vapour. Moisture condenses on your cold bathroom mirror, or out-of-doors, dew appears on cold rocks or plants. When cooling occurs in mid-air, the invisible vapour can turn into the tiny droplets of water that we see floating about as mist, clouds, or the 'steamy breath' from our hot damp lungs on a chilly day.

We talk about fog when the droplets make it difficult for us to see to do things. Pilots worry when visibility is under a kilometre; anything less than 200 m makes motoring difficult. Weather stations record visibility by keeping an eye on objects at known distances, noting the furthest to be seen. You could do this too, measuring the distances off a good map.

Damp air blown onto cooler upland

HILL FOG

Warmer lowland

Fog can happen in either windy or calm conditions. Particularly in spring and early summer when the sea is still cool, warm air can blow off the land and be chilled, giving coastal fog. Or damp air from a lowland area may be cooled by being blown up slopes, giving hill fog up there. But often fog happens on windless clear nights, down on the low ground itself. As the heat escapes into the clear sky from the ground, the air lying on it is chilled and a layer of fog builds up. Sometimes this is only waist deep, but whole valleys can fill up as cold heavy air drains in from the surrounding slopes. This kind is more common in the country than in towns because of heat from the houses, but cities have other problems. There, smoke and exhaust fumes can become mixed with fog. SMOG is the word used when SM-oke pollutes f-OG. It's not good for visibility, or health. London used to have 'pea-soup' fog in the days of coal fires, but now smog is worst in cities like Los Angeles. There four million cars put 12,000 tonnes of pollution into the air each day!

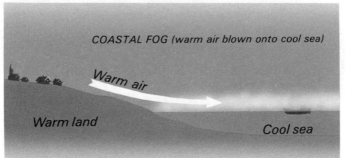

COASTAL FOG (warm air blown onto cool sea)

Warm air

Warm land

Cool sea

Fog is really a kind of cloud lying on the ground. Clouds are found at all heights from ground level right up to 10 or even 15 km above us. To 'get above the weather', airliners often fly at more than 12 km above the ground (40,000 ft or higher). Different kinds of clouds overlap in height, but when forecasters talk about Low Clouds, they generally mean ones with bases less than 2 km (7,000 ft) up; their Medium ones have bases from 2 km to about 8 km (25,000 ft); while the kinds that go highest begin from about 5 km (16,000 ft) to 13 km up. It's difficult to judge the heights of clouds from the ground, but often their character can give a clue. The highest are the Cirrus family. This means 'feathery', and they look like that

Cirrus

because it is so cold at their height that they are made up not of water droplets but of tiny ice crystals. Sometimes Cirrus clouds run like banners across the sky, and are

Cirro cumulus

called 'Mares' Tails'. If instead they have a bright dappled appearance like fish scales, that's called a 'Mackerel Sky'. On other occasions, the whole upper sky seems whitish because the crystals are more evenly spread, and they show up as haloes round the sun or moon. That's often a hint that the cloud layer may thicken, and that rain may soon come.

Happily for amateur forecasters, it is not often important to know heights exactly. The kind of cloud it is, and how the wind is moving it, often gives the best clue to the kind of weather that is coming – so note that in your weather diary.

Besides the 'feathery' Cirrus, the two main kinds of clouds are the 'heap clouds' of the Cumulus family, and the 'layer clouds' of the Stratus family.

Cirro stratus

Stratus

One of the main reasons why invisible water vapour becomes visible as clouds is that the air has risen to a cooler level in the sky. Where the wind is constantly stirring the air about, instead of clouds developing separately they blend into a sheet of Stratus, spreading across the sky like a bank of fog in mid-air. And like fog, a layer of Stratus can get thicker at night if the sky above the cloud is clear and more heat can escape from it out into space before sunrise.

The heaped-up Cumulus clouds however tend to grow by day, and disappear by night. This is because they are created by 'bubbles' of warm light air, rising from ground heated by the sun. As birds and glider pilots know, these 'thermals' can carry you thousands of metres up into the sky. When the rising air reaches a level that is too cold for it to hold its invisible water vapour, clouds begin to form. They have flattish bases at that height. The bubbles keep going upwards until they run out of energy, building fluffy domes like heaps of cottonwool.

There is usually clear sky between the separate Cumulus clouds, but quite often the two kinds blend together in a blurred lumpy layer. There's no problem in naming that in your weather diary: meteorologists simply call it 'Stratocumulus'!

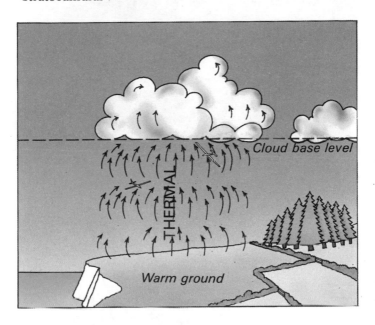

These are the words used for the Lower clouds. In order to identify the Medium height ones, Alto- is added to the names, giving *Alto*stratus and *Alto*cumulus.

The High versions are the Cirrus clouds we have already met: the Mares' Tails are plain Cirrus; *Cirro*cumulus is the proper name for Mackerel Sky, and *Cirro*stratus is the white layer that gives haloes. The other word that is worth learning is Nimbo-, because with either *Nimbo*stratus or Cumulo*nimbus* clouds, we are in for rain, or worse!

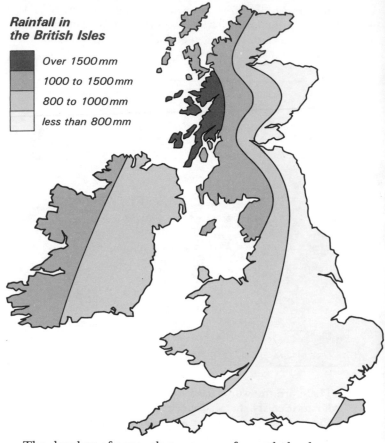

Rainfall in the British Isles

Over 1500 mm

1000 to 1500 mm

800 to 1000 mm

less than 800 mm

The droplets of water that we see as fog and cloud can stay floating in the air as long as they don't get too big and heavy – when that happens they fall as rain. Raindrops need to be about ½ mm across to fall, but they seldom go beyond 6 mm in diameter. Above that size, they tend to break up into smaller ones (which is just as well for us, since the large ones can hit the ground at around 8 m a second!). People have odd ideas about how much rain falls on them — many wouldn't believe that a day of misery can be produced by as little as half a centimetre of rain! And though many people think all of Britain is a rainy place, the amount that falls in different parts can vary from less than half a metre to more than 5 m in a year. There are great contrasts even within other small countries like New Zealand too, let alone across the vastnesses of Australia or North America. There, in some desert areas, no rain at all may fall for several years. Elsewhere there is heavy rain in certain seasons, with drought in between. In other places, there is hardly a day in the year without some drizzle, though the yearly total may not be high.

You can find out what really happens where you live by making your own rain gauge. Cut off the top of a plastic soft drinks bottle, and fit it upside down into the remainder as a funnel. Since the diameter of the entry is the same as the bottle, the depth of water caught will be the rainfall figure. If you use a wider funnel, compare the size of the top of the funnel with the base of the bottle: e.g. if the funnel is four times bigger, 40 mm in the bottle only means 10 mm of rainfall. Watch too where you set up the gauge. Although it mustn't be sheltered by overhanging trees or buildings, it shouldn't be in too exposed a place either,  since the wind can stop drops from settling into the funnel. But it must be high enough off the ground (or roof) to prevent extra water from splashing in, and firmly fixed so that it won't fall over.

If snow comes, you can measure how much has fallen with a ruler, though it can be difficult to find an even place where the wind has neither blown it away nor built up a drift. Because of the amount of air amongst snowflakes, 10 cm of snowfall only represents about as much water as 1 cm of rain. Snow starts in freezing clouds, when ice crystals stick to each other and fall. They build up their beautiful patterns because of the way that

Snow flakes under a magnifying glass, each one has a different structure.

the thin flakes vibrate as they shimmer down through the air. Try collecting some by letting them fall onto a cold mirror – they are worth looking at through a magnifying glass. Snow forms in a gentle way, but hail is quite different.

Hailstones are lumps of ice created by the violent currents inside a big Cumulonimbus cloud – the kind that often gives thunderstorms. Instead of dropping out of the bottom of the cloud, big raindrops are swept upwards towards the freezing top of the towering cloud. Up there

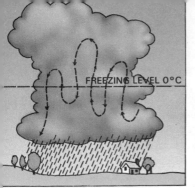

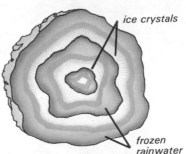

Section through a hailstone

ice crystals

frozen rainwater

The path a hailstone takes as it forms

they turn to ice, and gather a jacket of white ice crystals and snowflakes. Then their weight makes them fall, and as they drop through the lower part of the cloud they collect more water. If the upcurrents towards the base are really strong, before finally dropping free they may be caught and sent up over and over again. If you cut a big hailstone in half, you'll see that it's built up of successive layers of clear frozen rainwater and white ice crystals, telling the story of its 'yo-yo' movements. Though most hailstones are less than 5 mm across, some clouds produce ones big enough to beat down crops and even smash greenhouses. Pilots try to fly round big Cumulonimbus clouds rather than through them (some reach up over 10 km − 30,000 ft). It's not just because of hail damage. Even big airliners can be tossed around by the fierce air currents inside, and light aircraft have had their wings torn off. Besides that, there is the danger of lightning.

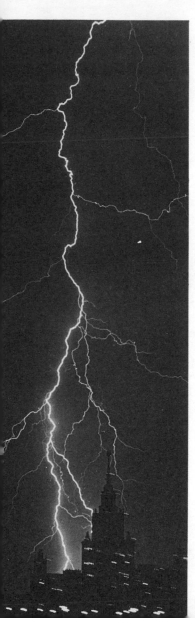

Lightning is caused by strong vertical currents inside a towering heap cloud. They split up the contents of the cloud, so that you get separate electric charges at the top and bottom of the cloud. Heavier droplets of water tend to stay nearer the bottom, while lighter ones are carried away towards the top. Heavy hailstones may throw off tiny spikes of ice which are light enough to go higher. Electric pressures of millions of volts build up, with positive charges in the freezing top of the cloud and negative ones in its wet base. When these charges become too great to be insulated by the air in between, there is a lightning flash. This may stay within the cloud, or strike right down to the earth beneath. As it makes its narrow and often forked channel through the air, for an instant the lightning releases great heat. The air affected expands explosively, then contracts again, giving the sound waves we call thunder. We see the flash instantaneously, but sound travels much more slowly than light, so if the

lightning is some way off, there is a pause between the flash and the thunderclap. If you count the number of seconds and divide by three, that gives the rough distance in kilometres.

Lightning conductor on a church tower

Many people are frightened by thunderstorms, and it is true that quite an ordinary one can release as much energy as several nuclear bombs. Certainly, there are risks. Since lightning is attracted to tall objects standing on their own, you should avoid sheltering under isolated trees. High buildings are protected with lightning conductors – strips of metal leading from their highest point directly to the ground. So, in a storm keep away from metal poles. Some golfers, caught in the open holding metal clubs, have been struck. Being inside a car gives very good protection. But the chance of being harmed is very slight, as you realise if you compare the tiny number of people killed in a year with the fact that round the earth nearly two thousand thunderstorms are going on at every moment.

Although hail and lightning are spectacular effects of uplifting by air currents, rain is a far commoner result of wet air being raised into colder parts of the sky. This lifting can happen in several ways besides in clouds of the Cumulus family, and the various ways give different kinds of rainy weather.

Forecasts often tell us to expect 'showers with bright intervals'. That is when the weathermen *do* expect Cumulus or Cumulonimbus clouds, with clear sky between them. As its upcurrents push the damp air high into the cold upper atmosphere, each cloud can release heavy rain. But since the individual clouds tend to be only a few kilometres across, it does not take them long to drift by on the wind, and each shower soon passes.

A different pattern results where wet air is cooled by being forced to rise when the wind hits a steep coastline or a range of hills. Cloud may form along the whole windward slope, with drizzle or steady rain for days on end. On the far side of the range, however, as the air descends and warms again, the clouds tend to disappear, giving a much drier area called a 'rain shadow'. Sometimes the descent warms the wind so much that it

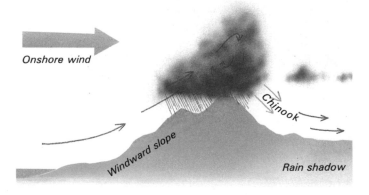

Onshore wind

Windward slope

Chinook

Rain shadow

can melt snow and shrivel vegetation. This effect, known by the Canadian name *Chinook*, usually needs steeply rising mountains to produce it. But the basic influence of slopes on rainfall is clear even in Britain, where hills facing into the prevailing winds off the Atlantic tend to be wetter than lowlands downwind to the east. The New Zealand Alps rise more abruptly than most British uplands. Four to six metres of water fall each year on their windward slopes, often leaving little more than a third of a metre for their dry side. Australia also has sharp contrasts between green coastal ranges and the deserts of the interior. In North America the Sierras and Rockies wall off the Pacific, helping to create inland deserts, hot in the south-west of the USA, and cold in the Canadian north-west.

Rainfall in New Zealand South Island

Over 5000 mm

2500 to 5000 mm

1500 to 2500 mm

1000 to 1500 mm

800 to 1000 mm

less than 800 mm

Not all the slopes up which damp air is pushed to give rain are made of rock, however. Warm air is often forced to rise when it meets colder heavier air. So damp air from the warmer parts of the oceans may run onto a ramp made up of the sloping edge of a mass of dense Polar air. Encounters of this kind can give belts of rain as much as 500 km wide and sometimes over 1,000 km long, and they are a very important part of the weather of Britain, New Zealand and parts of the Americas.

Some things that influence the climate, such as coastlines or mountains, certainly don't change their position or nature from day to day. But air masses can do just that, and it is their movements and changes that give the Earth much of the variety of its climates. They carry weather of different kinds from place to place. Those that come off oceans tend to be wet, and those from the interiors of continents dry, but whether they are cold or warm will depend on the regions that they came from. So you may hear forecasters talking of 'Polar Maritime' or 'Tropical Maritime' air masses, or 'Polar Continental' air, say, coming to affect you. It is not just the winds that we

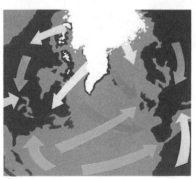

AIR MASSES   in Northern Hemisphere   in Southern Hemisphere

☐ Arctic   ☐ Polar Continental   ■ Polar Maritime

☐ Tropical Maritime   ☐ Tropical Continental

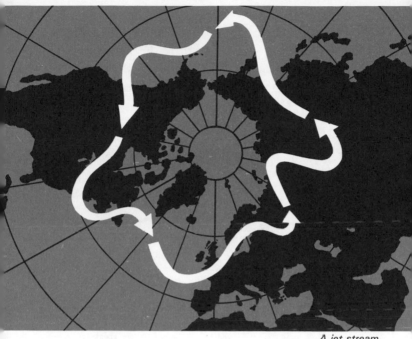

A jet stream

feel down at ground level that are involved in bringing
them. High in the sky there are narrow fast-flowing 'rivers
of air', which pilots call *jet streams*. Sometimes these
move at over 300 kph, and their pattern can alter quite
quickly. They help to make the weather so variable in
places like Britain or New Zealand, lying where several
types of air mass often meet and compete with each other.
Very much less variable climates are found in parts of the
world dominated by just one kind of air mass throughout
the year (say the cold Polar air of the Arctic, or the hot
wet air of the Equatorial rain forest regions). Elsewhere,
as in the Monsoon lands of India, different air masses
take strict turns in regular seasonal changes.

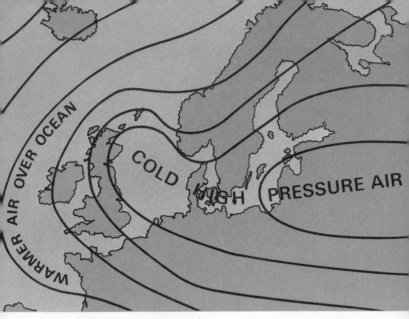

An anticyclone reaching out from the Continent towards Britain

In most parts of the world, a mass of high pressure air
(called an *anticyclone* or *high*) brings a period when the
weather does not change much. But whether that is good
or bad news depends on the time of year. For example, in
both winter and summer, because the high pressure keeps
out wet winds from the Atlantic, anticyclones tend to give
dry settled weather in Britain. But in winter, it can
become unpleasantly cold under an anticyclone. The
heavy chilled air spreads out from Scandinavia and
Russia, where the land cools down much more than the
sea during the continental winter. It stops the usual flow
of warmish air off the ocean, so Britain gets colder and
colder day by day. Frost is common. There may be
widespread freezing fogs, and the sky becomes covered
in a grey overcast. Sometimes this dense air mass lingers
for weeks, giving a dry but unusually severe winter.
1962/3 was the coldest winter in England since 1743, then

1978/9 brought the lowest temperatures recorded for two hundred years in many parts of northern Europe. In the summertime however, high pressure over Britain often gives a run of fine calm weather, ideal for holidays. There may be mist in the mornings because the clear skies allow the ground to cool at night, but it soon lifts as the sun shines down through the clear air above.

During a winter anticyclone

A lot of the most changeable weather in both the north and south halves of the world is associated with the opposites of these 'anticyclonic highs'. These are areas of low pressure air generally called *depressions*, or simply *lows* (the word *cyclone* is sometimes used too, to match *anticyclone*, but that's rather confusing, since cyclone is also used for the tropical storms like hurricanes). Depressions sometimes drift over the Atlantic on roughly a weekly rhythm, so there is some truth in the notion that once it starts to rain at weekends, the British may be stuck with the miseries of wet weekends for quite a while...

Summer anticyclones bring good weather for harvest

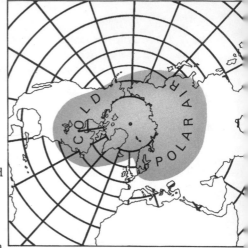

What makes a depression happen? Imagine looking down from a satellite high above the North Pole. The whole Arctic region is capped with its heavy cold Polar air mass. Then further south this is surrounded by warmer air. Where different air masses meet like this, meteorologists call the boundary between them a *front*. There is a line of fronts running round the planet there. But it isn't a simple line. It is affected by the differences in heating between the continents and oceans that it passes over, and by the changing routes of the high level jet stream winds. So it's not surprising that waves often develop in the line between the cold high pressure and the warm low pressure air. And in the northern half

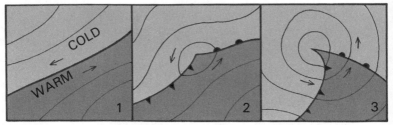

A wave tightens into the swirl of a depression

of the planet, the spinning of the Earth tends to make winds turn clockwise as they blow outwards from high pressure, and anti-clockwise as they are drawn into lows. As usual, the spin goes the opposite way in the southern hemisphere. With air currents passing each other in opposite directions like that, a wave often develops into a great swirl circling round a centre of low pressure where it has swept in a tongue of lighter warm air. That's what we call the 'depression'.

As we have seen, clouds develop along the boundaries between this 'warm sector' air and the colder air around it, where the warm wet air is forced upwards over the sloping edges of the denser cold air. Nowadays, weather satellites show us the swirling patterns in the clouds, helping forecasters to see where the centres of depressions are, and to know just where their fronts between warm and cold air will affect the weather.

WEATHER BELTS
MOVING THIS WAY

CLEAR SKIES

CUMULONIMBUS

CUMULUS

COLD
AIR

STRATUS

WARM AIR

NARROW RAIN BELT

The warm sector of a depression passes over

Meteorologists talk about 'warm' and 'cold' fronts. When a warm air mass is advancing and replacing colder air, people on the ground will feel the temperature rise as the front passes over them. So that kind is called a 'warm front'. But where a cold air mass is pushing in under warmer air, they feel chillier as the 'cold front' arrives. You can get rain along both kinds, but the weather that they bring follows rather different patterns. This is because where dense cold air is pushing into a warm air mass, the cold front often forms a fairly steep 'wall' in the sky, so things happen quite quickly as it sweeps past. But events build up more slowly as a warm front approaches, because there the warm air is riding up the much more gently sloping 'ramp' that you get at the back of retreating cold air.

So let's see what happens to the weather when a warm wet air mass moves over your home. Before it arrives, you are in cool dry conditions with clear skies. The first

WEATHER BELTS
MOVING THIS WAY

CLEAR SKIES

NIMBOSTRATUS

ALTO
STRATUS

CIRRUS

COLD AIR

'RAMP' OF RETREATING COLD AIR

WIDE RAIN BELT

warning that wet air is on the way may be Mares' Tails
Cirrus, very high in the sky. Then the clouds slowly
thicken and get lower as the ramp of the warm front
gradually passes overhead, until most of the sky is covered
with Stratus clouds – first Cirrostratus, then Altostratus
and Nimbostratus, getting lower and lower. It is because
of the wideness of the gently sloping ramp that the rain
belt is often as much as 500 km wide. The heaviest rain
falls as the part of the front touching the ground passes.
But then the temperature rises, the clouds thin and (with
luck!) the rain stops as the warm air mass sweeps over
you. Within a day or so, or even a few hours, more cold
air will arrive. Because of the greater steepness of the cold
front, there is less warning. But the steepness also means
that the rain belt is narrower. So although there is often
really heavy rain from big Cumulonimbus clouds along a
cold front, the period with continuous rain tends to be
short. Soon you are into clearer cool weather again, with
just showers from Cumulus clouds drifting by.

The series of events that we've just looked at tend to be repeated every time we get depressions passing over us. So though the weather in places like Britain and New Zealand and the parts of North America affected by depressions is certainly 'changeable', that's not the same as 'unpredictable'. And this is why by using simple instruments and keeping track of the pattern of events in a weather diary you can become a real forecaster.

WEATHER BELTS MOVING THIS WAY

CLEAR

CUMULONIMBUS

COLD HIGH PRESSURE AIR

STRATUS

CUMULUS

WARMER LOWER PRESSURE

RAIN

pressure rises   *cold*   *warm*   *pressure low but steadier*

What your weather diary shows as the warm sector of a depression passes over

You'll remember that since cold air is heavy it gives high pressure, while warmer air is lighter. So if you watch your barometer and find that pressure keeps falling for several hours and the clouds are getting lower, then you can suspect a warm front is coming nearer with its rain. As it passes you, and the 'warm sector' of the depression moves over you, the barometer should steady off at a low reading while the thermometer shows a rise. You can tell when the cold front is arriving with its heavy dense air, because the pressure will go up quite sharply as the temperature falls.

Even without instruments, you can do quite well. For example, note not just the kinds of clouds but the way that they move. We've seen that air moving from high to low pressure is sent swirling by the spinning of the Earth. The swirl of air round the 'low' at the centre of a depression gives the winds that we feel (or our wind vane shows), down near the ground. But the depression with its whole pattern of weather moves over us because it is being

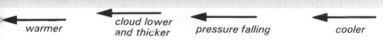

**WEATHER BELTS
MOVING THIS WAY**

CLEAR

CIRRUS

**ALTO
STRATUS**

NIMBOSTRATUS

COLD HIGH PRESSURE AIR

AIR

RAIN

warmer *cloud lower
and thicker* *pressure falling* *cooler*

swept along by winds prevailing higher up in the atmosphere. The upper clouds carried by these high-up winds often move at right angles to the wind at ground level. Put your back to the wind that you feel, and if the upper clouds come from your *right*, the weather will usually become all *right* too. If they come from your left, the weather is likely to get worse (remember the Latin name for left is *sinister*...). That works in northern lands. If you live in the southern hemisphere, you have to face *into* the wind there for the rule to work, since the swirl goes the other way.

Satellite photograph of a depression approaching the British Isles

Meteorologists make maps which bring together information gathered every hour from many weather stations on the ground, and from ships, aircraft and satellites. On these charts they plot information on pressure, winds, temperature, humidity, clouds, visibility — and what the weather actually is and recently has been at each place. The result is fairly complicated, but some of the signs that they use also appear in the simpler Weather Maps on TV and in newspapers, so it is worth being able to recognise them.

Fronts are shown by heavy lines, with 'teeth' on the side they are moving towards. Sharp teeth indicate a cold front, and rounded ones a warm front. If both kinds of teeth are shown on the same line, this means that the cold front has overtaken the warm front, and lifted the warm air right off the ground (you may hear this called an *occluded* front). The weather it gives fits with what it is — a combination of warm and cold front. So first the clouds get lower, then after some continuous rain the skies clear

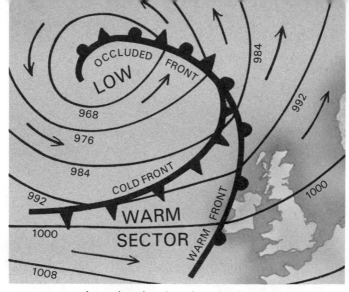

Labels on the chart: OCCLUDED FRONT, LOW, 968, 976, 984, 992, 1000, 1008, COLD FRONT, WARM SECTOR, WARM FRONT, 984, 992, 1000

A weather chart based on the depression photograph shown opposite

quickly, with scattered showers.

Isobars are the other main thing shown. *Iso-* means 'equal', and *bar* (as in *bar*ometer) indicates 'pressure', so these are lines drawn on the map to show where the pressure is the same — just as contours on a map of hills show where the land is the same height. On an isobar map, the 'hills' are the areas where barometers show that the pressure is high, and the 'hollows' are the low pressure areas such as the centres of depressions.

Satellite photograph of a depression over the Antarctic Ocean — the swirl goes the opposite way in the southern hemisphere

49

Although forecasting is now more a matter of science than witchcraft, even in the 20th century we can't claim much real *control* over our planet's weather. Compared to our irrigation or frost protection schemes, the amounts of natural energy involved are immense. Remember that even small thunderstorms equal atom bombs, and the effect of the sun on the ground can be as much as a million 1 kw electric fires per square kilometre! Even if we

Computer room in an international meteorological office

were able to do things like deliberately melting the Polar ice by nuclear power, the way weather systems affect each other is so complicated that it is difficult to be sure a change for the better in one region might not be disastrous elsewhere.

We may not have proper control, but many things we do without any deliberate intention of altering the atmosphere *are* affecting it. These range from the cutting down of vast tropical rain forests, or the production of carbon dioxide gas from coal and oil fuels, to such unlikely things as the use of aerosol cans. It is difficult to recognise effects from our own actions because natural changes are going on too, all the time. The weather patterns of the Earth are changing not only from day to day, and season to season, but year to year and through centuries. Another Ice Age seems due in a few thousand years, but some scientists think our carbon dioxide pollution may have prevented it.

Meteosat – a satellite used in weather forecasting

So, though we can become quite successful at forecasting tomorrow's local weather even using simple instruments, it is very much more complicated to look farther into the future. But with satellites and computers among their tools, meteorologists are developing a whole new understanding of how our planet's weather works. One forecast that we can be sure of is that there are still interesting discoveries ahead of us.

Index